Long Long Ago

Long Long Ago

ROBIN SKELTON

Illustrations by
PAMELA BREEZE CURRIE

RONSDALE PRESS
1996

LONG LONG AGO
Copyright Text © 1996 Robin Skelton
Copyright Illustrations © 1996 Pamela Breeze Currie

RONSDALE PRESS
3350 West 21st Avenue
Vancouver, BC, Canada
V6S 1G7

Set in Sabon 13 on 16
Typesetting: The Typeworks, Vancouver, BC
Printing: Hignell Printing, Winnipeg, Manitoba
Cover Art: Pamela Breeze Currie
Cover Design: Cecilia Jang
Author Photo Credit: Jane Tuohy

The publisher wishes to thank the Canada Council and the British Columbia Cultural Services Branch for their financial assistance.

CANADIAN CATALOGUING-IN-PUBLICATION DATA

Skelton, Robin, 1925–
   Long long ago
   ISBN 0-921870-36-1
   I. Currie, Pamela II. Title.
PS8537.K38L66   1996   jC813'.54   C95-911126-3
PZ7.S53Lo   1996

Seven Stories

The Story
of the Ostrich

In the beginning of things the Ostrich was the greediest and most conceited of birds. He had big, strong wings of which he was very proud, and whenever there was any food to be had, he flew very quickly indeed and got there before anyone else, so that when all the birds arrived, they found that there was nothing left for them. The Ostrich had eaten it all!

All the birds were very cross about this but did not know what they could do, for when they complained, the Ostrich would laugh and say proudly, "Why don't you grow stronger wings, then you could get there first? I have the biggest and strongest wings in the whole wide world, and I need a great deal of food to keep them strong, so it is only right that I should eat more food than anyone else."

At last they decided that something must be done, and met together in a quiet place in the forest to see what they could arrange.

The Yellowhammer, who had very short wings, and so hardly ever got any food at all, said, "We should clip the

Ostrich's wings." But the Ostrich was so big and strong that no one could think how it could be managed.

Then the Sparrow suggested that they should imprison the Ostrich in a cage and so prevent him from eating more than his share of food, but again nobody could suggest a way of doing it. Just as they were all beginning to think that there was no way of solving the problem, the Jackdaw said, "I have a plan. Leave it all to me, and you will see that soon the Ostrich will stop being such a nuisance."

"What is the plan, Jackdaw?" asked all the birds, but the Jackdaw would not tell them, and would only say mysteriously, "Wait and see," and flew away leaving everybody very puzzled and curious indeed.

The Jackdaw flew through the forest till he came to the Rabbit's burrow, and knocked on the door of the burrow, and the Rabbit let him in, and the two creatures talked together for a long time. When the Jackdaw flew away again he was laughing, "Haark, harrk, haark," and the Rabbit, as he waved goodbye, was looking mischievous.

The very next day the Ostrich was walking along the path through the forest when whom should he meet but the Rabbit.

"Good morning, Ostrich," said the Rabbit. "How are you today?"

"I am very well, Rabbit," said the Ostrich. "How are you?"

"I am a little tired today," said the Rabbit, "for yesterday I went to visit a cousin of mine a long way from here, and I did not go to bed as early as usual. My cousin and I had an argument which may interest you. He said that a bird-friend of his had the biggest and strongest wings in the world, and I said that you had."

"You are quite right, Rabbit," said the Ostrich. "I have the biggest and strongest wings in the whole wide world, except, perhaps, for the great Eagle."

"My cousin said that his bird-friend had a race with the Eagle, and beat him," said the Rabbit, "so perhaps he was right after all—, but then he had magic feathers which my cousin had given him, so perhaps it was not a fair race."

"That seems likely," said the Ostrich. "If I had magic feathers in my wings I am sure that I could fly farther and faster than both the Eagle and your cousin's friend, though it seems to me that I might be able to beat them in a race as things are at present, if I tried hard enough, for my wings are very big and strong. Where did your cousin get the magic feathers?" he added, trying not to sound too curious.

"It is a great secret which you must promise to keep," answered the Rabbit. "My cousin knows a very wise gnome who lives in a cave deep below the surface of the earth, and in his cave he has a magic garden. Anything that is planted in this garden will grow a hundred times bigger and stronger. My cousin took the wing feathers of his friend and asked the gnome to plant them in this garden, and he did, and they grew and grew and grew until they were bigger and stronger than any other feathers in the whole wide world. Then my cousin took them back to his friend. That is how he managed to beat even the great Eagle in a race and why my cousin thought (though I think he was wrong) that you were not the biggest and strongest bird in the world anymore."

"Do you know where this cave is?" asked the Ostrich eagerly.

"My cousin told me," said the Rabbit.

"Do you suppose that the gnome would plant any of my feathers in his garden?" said the Ostrich.

"I could ask him for you," said the Rabbit. "As a matter of fact I am going to see him today to ask him to grow my cousin some lettuce, for my cousin is very busy and cannot go himself. I will be home again before tea-time, and could tell you what he says."

"Thank you very much, Rabbit," said the Ostrich. He flapped his huge wings and flew away thinking of all the food he would get when he could fly even farther and faster than he could at that time, and saying to himself, "Even the great Eagle will have to look up to me then. I shall be the strongest bird in the whole wide world."

At tea-time that afternoon the Ostrich went to call on Rabbit. He was too big to get inside the burrow, so he knocked on the door with his claws, and stood outside waiting. After a few moments the Rabbit opened the door and said, "Hello Ostrich."

"Hello Rabbit," said the Ostrich. "Have you seen the Magician, and will he plant my feathers in his garden?"

"Yes," said the Rabbit. "You must come with me to a lonely place and give me your feathers, and I will take them to him straight away."

So the Ostrich and the Rabbit went together to a lonely place at the edge of the forest where it was very sandy and there were a lot of rabbit burrows and other holes in the ground, and the Ostrich pulled out all his wing feathers with his beak and gave them to Rabbit. He felt rather cold without them, but he said to himself, "Soon I shall have the biggest and strongest wings in the whole wide world, and even the great Eagle will admire me," and he felt proud and important.

"How soon will you come back with the magic feathers?" he asked the Rabbit.

"When they are a hundred times stronger and bigger than they are now, and not a moment before," Rabbit replied and he vanished down the nearest hole with the feathers in his arms.

The next day the Ostrich called at the Rabbit's burrow, but the Rabbit was not at home, and so the Ostrich had to go away again without his new feathers. The day after that the Ostrich called again, but still the Rabbit was not to be found. The third day the Ostrich met the Rabbit in the forest and asked him where the feathers were.

"They are not ready yet, Ostrich," said the Rabbit. "The gnome says he does not know how long they will take to grow as he has never planted any feathers quite as big as yours before."

And that was the last the Ostrich ever saw of the Rabbit. And that is why, to this day, the Ostrich has such small wings and cannot fly, and that is why, also, he pokes his head into the sand.

He is looking to see if the Rabbit is returning with his magic feathers so that he can fly away. But he never is.

The Story of the Owl
and the Crocodile

One day, a very, very long time ago, all the animals and birds and other creatures in the world met together to talk about their troubles.

A great many of them did not know how to read or write, and some of the birds were even not quite sure how to build their nests properly. The Rabbit, who was very fond of lettuce, found that whenever he planted it in his garden it died, and the Monkey was often very ill indeed because of eating bad nuts.

After a great deal of talk, the Jackdaw suggested that they needed someone wise enough to tell them all the things they did not know, and who could teach the birds how to build nests, and show the Monkey which nuts he should not eat.

"But the only person who knows all these things," said the Jackdaw, "is the old Magician who lives in the cave at the end of the world, and he is a long way away and never comes to visit us."

"Let us send someone to his cave, then," suggested the Rabbit, "to ask him for the gift of wisdom."

All the creatures thought this was a very good idea, but could not agree who should be the messenger. At last, after a great deal of thought, the Monkey said, "We should send two creatures—the Crocodile because he lives in the river and could teach all the fishes in the river as well as the birds and animals that live on the bank, and the Owl because he can fly quickly from place to place and meet all the birds as well as the animals. Also, they are both fairly wise already, so they will not have as much to learn as other creatures."

Everybody thought this a good idea, and so the very next day the Crocodile and the Owl set off on their long journey to the cave at the end of the world where the Magician lived.

They travelled for a long, long time, the Crocodile walking on the ground or swimming in the rivers, and the Owl flying ahead and then returning to tell him which way he should go, for the Owl, being in the air, could see the path more clearly than the Crocodile. Each night they would find a comfortable place to sleep, the Owl a tall tree and the Crocodile a soft bed

of mud at the edge of a pool or river, and each day they would wake up very early and travel until it was dark.

They crossed the rivers and mountains and went through thick jungles and huge forests; they sailed across seas on a raft the Crocodile made, for the seas were too wide for the Crocodile to swim or the Owl to fly across; they journeyed through sandy deserts and countries where there was snow all the year round, and sometimes they were very hot and sometimes very cold, and they were often very tired indeed.

After they had travelled such a long time that they could not count the days and nights since they last saw their homes, they came at last to the End of the World, and there, in the side of the biggest mountain they had ever seen, was the Magician's cave, and the Magician sitting outside it, reading a book of spells in the bright sunlight.

"Hello," said the Magician kindly. "You have come a very

long way, and must be tired. Come into the cave and have a cup of cocoa and tell me what I can do for you."

So the Owl and Crocodile went into the cave and had a lovely, hot, steaming cup of cocoa, and told the Magician that they had come to ask him for the gift of Wisdom so that they could help all the other creatures in their troubles, and teach the birds how to build better nests and the Monkey how to avoid eating bad nuts.

"You are asking a very difficult thing," said the Magician, "but I think I have a spell that will help you. You must do everything I tell you, and be very careful not to make any mistakes, or the spell will not work, and you must not disobey me in anything or you will be punished."

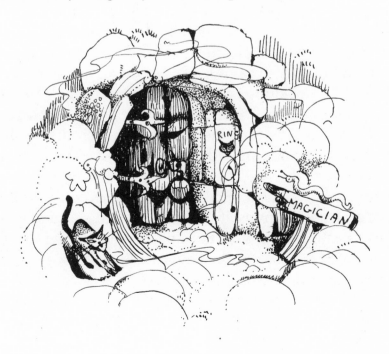

The Owl and the Crocodile agreed to do as they were told, so the Magician sent them out of the cave and began to mix up all kinds of magical powders and herbs in a huge cauldron, and all the time he muttered spells over them which he read from his big book. After a while he went to the mouth of the cave and called for the Owl.

"You must come into the cave," he said, "but remember! Do everything I tell you, or you will have misfortune."

The Owl went into the cave, and the Magician told him to stand facing the wall with his back to the magic cauldron, and not to turn his head to try to see what the Magician was doing, "For if you turn your head," said the Magician, "the spell will go wrong and you will be punished."

The Owl stood staring at the wall for a long time, and could hear the Magician behind him muttering spells, and the big iron spoon clinking against the sides of the cauldron as he stirred the magical mixture. He wondered very much what the Magician was doing, and when the muttering and the stirring stopped and all was silent, he became very curious indeed. He wanted to turn his head and watch the spell being made, but the Magician had told him not to, and so he stood still, staring at the wall of the cave, getting more and more curious as the minutes went by. At last he could bear it no longer, and said to himself, "The Magician said I was not to turn my head, but he said nothing about looking out of the corners of my eyes." So he moved his eyes away from the wall and peeped out of their corners to see what was going on, but all he saw was a cloud of grey smoke, and just as he had turned his eyes back to the wall feeling very puzzled and disappointed, the Magician said, "It is all over. You may turn round now," and there was the cauldron and the Magician just as they were before, and the Owl went out into the sunlight wondering what had happened.

Then the Crocodile was called into the cave, and was told, like Owl, to stand facing the wall with his back to the cauldron, and not to try to see what the Magician was doing, "For if you turn your eyes and peep out of the corners of them to see what is going on," said the Magician, "the spell will go wrong, and you will be punished."

The Crocodile stood staring at the wall for a long time, and could hear the Magician muttering and the iron spoon clinking, and wondered very much what the Magician was doing. Then the clinking and the muttering stopped, and all was silent, and the Crocodile, like the Owl, became very curious indeed. At last he said to himself, "The Magician said I was not to move my eyes and peep out of the corners of them, but he

said nothing about turning my head." So, looking straight in front of him, and without moving his eyes at all, he slowly turned his head and looked where he had seen the cauldron and the Magician, but all he saw was a cloud of grey smoke, and just as he had turned his head back again he heard a voice say, "It's

all over. You may turn around now," and there were the cauldron and the Magician just as they were before, and the
Crocodile went out into the sunlight wondering what had happened.

Then the Magician came out of the cave and said to them,
"The spell has worked, and as soon as you reach your homes
you will find that you have the gift of Wisdom, and are able
to help all the other creatures in their troubles and teach them
what they need to know. But both of you tried to see what I
was doing in the cave and so must be punished. Although the
Owl did as he was told and did not turn his head, he peeped
out of the corner of his eyes, and as a result, from this time
forward he shall never be able to move his eyes again. The
Crocodile did as he was told and did not move his eyes, but
he turned his head, and so the punishment is that from this
time forward he shall never be able to turn his head again.
Although both of you did what you were told, you both tried
to see what I was doing, which you knew you should not
have done. You have been very naughty indeed." And the
Magician went back into his cave and the Owl and the
Crocodile never saw him again.

And so, to this very day, the Owl, though he can turn his
head almost right round, cannot move his eyes, and the
Crocodile, though he can move his eyes very easily and see a
great deal out of the corners of them, cannot turn his head.

But they are both very wise.

The Story of
the Jackdaw

 Long, long ago, in the very beginning of things, the Jackdaw was the only bird without a wife, and he was very lonely. Everywhere he went he saw the other birds with their wives, building nests and singing happily together, and each day he felt more lonely than he did the day before.

At last he could bear it no longer, and went to ask the wise Owl what he should do to get himself a wife. "All the birds have wives," said the Owl, "and so there must be one for you somewhere. You must look for her, for perhaps she is lost in the forest and cannot find you."

So the Jackdaw flew through the forest looking for his wife, and asking everybody he met if he had seen her. He met the Rabbit first of all, and said to him, "Rabbit, have you seen my wife anywhere, please?" but the Rabbit was busy painting the front of his burrow, and said crossly, "I am too busy to be bothered by stupid questions. You haven't got a wife, so how can I have seen her?" and the Jackdaw flew miserably away. Then he met the Camel and asked him, but the

Camel was half asleep in the sun, and only said dreamily, "No, no, no, no, no…" and paid very little attention to Jackdaw's unhappiness. The Horse was more helpful, but said that he had not seen the Jackdaw's wife either, though he promised to keep a look-out for her. The Bullfrog and the Ostrich were both too proud to listen to what the Jackdaw was saying. Not one of the creatures the Jackdaw met could help him.

At last the Jackdaw grew very tired indeed, and sat down on a branch of a tree overhanging the river and began to cry. He had only sobbed once or twice, when a voice from the mud at the edge of the river said suddenly, "What's the matter Jackdaw?" It was the Crocodile.

Now the Crocodile is very wise, as you know, but also rather mischievous, so when he heard the Jackdaw's story, he said solemnly, "You must make one!"

"I beg your pardon?" said the Jackdaw.

"I said you must make one," said the Crocodile. "You have not got a wife, and you want a wife, so you must try to make one."

"But what shall I make one of?" asked the Jackdaw.

"Why what do you think?" said the Crocodile. "Black straw of course!" and before the Jackdaw had time to ask him where any black straw was to be found, he had slipped into the river, and swum away.

So the Jackdaw began to search for some black straw, but he could not find any anywhere. He flew all over the forest asking people where he could get some black straw. He asked the Rabbit, but the Rabbit was busy planting a rose tree beside his newly painted front door, and would not pay any attention. The Camel was fast asleep in the sun, and the Jackdaw could not wake him. And the horse, though he tried very hard to think where some black straw could be found, was not able to help Jackdaw either. And so for a very long time the Jackdaw flew about the forest crying, "Has anyone seen any black straw? Black straw? Has anyone seen black

straw?" But nobody ever had, and he grew tired and very miserable indeed.

One day, after he had asked all the creatures he knew where he could get some black straw, and no one could tell him, he was sitting on the branch of a tree overlooking the river, when he happened to look down into the water. And there, as clear as clear could be, was another Jackdaw just like himself. With a cry of "black straw" the Jackdaw flew down towards it, but when he touched the water the other bird disappeared, and the strong current of the river swept him along gasping for breath, and swallowing a great deal of cold water, until he was nearly drowned. But in the end, just as he was thinking that his last moment had come, the river washed him, more dead than alive, up onto an island, and he lay there quite exhausted and fell fast asleep.

When he woke up he found that he had a dreadful cold, but he staggered to his feet and flew away, still crying, in a very hoarse voice, "Black Straw! Black Straw! Black Straw! Black Straw! Has anyone seen Black Straw?"

Just as luck would have it, a lady Jackdaw, who had been lost in the forest near the river, heard him, and flew to meet him, and so the Jackdaw found his wife at last. And he called her, as you might suppose, Black Straw, and they lived happily together ever after. But from that very day the Jackdaw has had a hoarse voice, and he is even now very worried whenever he loses sight of his wife, so that to this very day if you see a lonely Jackdaw flying about you will hear him calling for her in a very hoarse voice, "Black Straw, Black Straw, Black, Black, Black! Has anybody seen Black Straw?"

The Story of

the Kingfisher,

the Nightingale,

and the Magpie

 One day in the very beginning of things, when magic was still alive and all the animals and birds were friendly with one another, the old Magician who lived in the cave at the End of the World discovered he had lost his magic diamond ring. The day before he had been to a party with the four winds, and he decided he must have dropped it then, without noticing.

He had travelled a very long way with the winds and it could have fallen almost anywhere on earth, so he called the Hummingbird to him (for the Hummingbird, as you know, was the Magician's messenger) and told him to tell all the birds and animals that whoever found the ring and brought it back to him could have his dearest wish granted as a reward. So the Hummingbird flew to the homes of all the animals and birds and other creatures, and everyone began to search for the ring.

They searched for days and days. The Rabbit and the Mole and the Badger looked in all the holes in the ground to see if the ring had fallen there, and the fishes looked on the bed of the sea and in all the rivers, and the birds flew from tree to tree to see if it had been caught in any of the branches; but no one could find it.

The Mole was the first to give up the search. "For," he said, "my eyes are very dim, and I have looked for it everywhere I can think of, and if it is found now it is sure to be by someone with brighter eyes than mine."

And then the Giraffe stopped looking for it. "For," he said, "I have looked everywhere I can think of, and I am sure it will never be found again."

And gradually all the animals and birds and other creatures stopped looking for the ring and went back to their homes and asked the Hummingbird to tell the Magician that the ring was lost for ever—all, that is, but the Kingfisher and the Nightingale, and they went on searching for it, day after day, for a very long time indeed.

At last one morning the Nightingale was flying over a stream when she saw a gleam of light in the pebbles near the bank, and flew down to see what it was, and there, right at the bottom of the stream, was the ring, shining up at her. The Nightingale did not know how to get the ring, for she could not swim, but just then up flew the Kingfisher.

"Good morning," said the Kingfisher, "have you found the ring yet?"

"Good morning, Kingfisher," said the Nightingale. "Yes, I have just found it this very minute, but it is lying at the bottom of the stream and I cannot swim and so do not know how to get it."

"I cannot swim myself," said the Kingfisher, "but I often dive into the water and fly out again. Perhaps, if I hold my breath for a very long time I can dive deep enough to get it, and then you can take it to the Magician, and get the reward."

"If you get it for me," said the Nightingale, "we will share the reward."

So the Kingfisher stood on a branch of a tree overhanging the stream, and took a deep breath, and dived into the stream. The water was cold and the stream deep, and the Kingfisher

was very frightened, but he dived so cleverly that he reached the bottom of the stream at the very place where the ring was lying, and grabbed it in his long beak, and, beating his wings very quickly, rose to the surface. When he reached the surface the Nightingale held out her claw and helped him on to the bank, and they were both very excited and happy, though the Kingfisher was wet and tired and cold. By this time it was growing dark, and it was too late for them to return the ring to the Magician that day, so the Nightingale invited the

Kingfisher to come home with her and have a hot drink and go to bed so that he would not catch a cold, and then they would both take the ring back to the Magician the next day.

When they reached the Nightingale's home, however, and had had their hot drink, they were much too excited to go to bed, and began to talk of the wishes they would ask the Magician to grant them.

"I have always wanted," said the Kingfisher, looking down at his shabby brown feathers, "a really beautiful coat, blue and green and shining. I shall ask for that."

"I don't want a new coat," said the Nightingale, "though mine is just as shabby as yours, but I have always wanted to be able to sing as sweetly as my friends the Thrush and Blackbird. I think I will ask the Magician to give me a beautiful voice."

"It would be fun to be able to sing beautifully, I agree," said the Kingfisher, "but I would much rather have a new coat so that all the other birds should admire me, for at present they are very rude to me about my shabby feathers."

As they were both talking in this way, the Magpie, who was flying past the Nightingale's nest, heard them, and stopped to listen, for he was a very curious bird. He heard the Nightingale say, "Thank you very much for helping me, Kingfisher," and the Kingfisher reply, "*You* found the ring, you know. That was the most difficult thing to do. Thank you very much for letting me share in the reward."

"Aha!" thought the Magpie, "they have found the magic ring," and he peeped inside the nest and saw that the Kingfisher and the Nightingale had fallen asleep, and that the ring was lying beside them on the floor of the nest, shining very brightly in the moonlight.

Very cautiously and quietly the Magpie tiptoed into the nest and picked up the ring in his beak and crept out again without waking the two sleeping birds.

"Now I have the ring," he said to himself, "but I will not take it straight back to the Magician, for it is a magic ring; I will see if I can work some magic with it first."

So he flew to a very lonely place, and put the ring on one of his legs, and tried to think of something he could wish for. He was not a very clever bird, however, and could only think of wishing for a beautiful voice and a new coat, the two things he had heard the Nightingale and the Kingfisher discussing. So he said in a very clear voice, "O Magic Ring, give me a beautiful voice and a new coat of red and yellow." He was not a polite bird at all, and so did not say "please." There was a flash of lightning, and he looked down at his feathers and saw that they were red and yellow, and opened his beak and heard himself singing as sweetly as a Thrush, and he was pleased and proud, and strutted in the moonlight, admiring his new coat, and singing very loudly indeed. Then he went home to bed, with the ring still on his leg, deciding that he would take the ring back to the Magician only after he had thought of some more wishes he would like to be granted.

The next morning the Kingfisher and Nightingale awoke and could not find the ring anywhere. They were very miserable indeed, and cried bitterly. Just as they were saying to each other that someone must have stolen it, who should come flying by but the Magpie, looking very pleased with himself.

"Look at my new coat," he cried. But though Kingfisher and Nightingale looked very hard indeed his coat looked to them just the same as ever.

"Listen to my beautiful singing," said the Magpie, but when he opened his beak all they heard was the chattering noise that the Magpie usually made.

"Your coat is the same colour, and your voice is as harsh as usual," said the Kingfisher. "You may think they are different, but they are not."

"You are very stupid," said the Magpie. "I found the Magician's ring, and wished for a new coat and a beautiful voice, and my wishes were granted."

"We found the ring," said the Nightingale, "and you must have stolen it from us."

"And your wishes have not been granted," said the Kingfisher. "You have been bewitched as a punishment. Once you take off the ring you will see that you are just the same as you always were."

So the Magpie took off the ring and looked at his feathers, and they were no longer red and yellow but their old black and white, and he opened his beak to sing, but found he could only chatter. Then he said, "I shall take the ring back to the Magician and tell him that I found it, and then I will have a real new coat and a beautiful voice," and flew away with the ring in his beak, and the Kingfisher and the Nightingale flew after him.

They all arrived at the Magician's cave very quickly, for the winds, who were the Magician's friends, helped them, and made them fly ten times as fast as usual, and when they got there the Magpie took the ring to the Magician and said, "Here is the ring. Give me a new coat and a beautiful voice as my reward."

The Nightingale and the Kingfisher were very shy and did not say anything, but only looked sad and disappointed.

"You may have your reward," said the Magician, "but what do the Kingfisher and the Nightingale want?"

"They pretend that they found the ring," said the Magpie,

"but of course they didn't. And they have come to try to get the reward for themselves."

"I see," said the Magician, and then he turned to the two birds and asked them what they had to say, and they told him the whole story. "I can soon find out which of you is speaking the truth," said the Magician, "for the ring will tell me." And he put the ring on his finger and looked into the diamond and it showed him, first a picture of the Nightingale finding the ring, then a picture of the Kingfisher diving into the stream, and then a picture of the Magpie stealing away from the Nightingale's nest with the ring in his beak.

"Now I know the truth," said the Magician, "and all three will have your rewards. What would you like to have?" he said, turning to the Nightingale.

"I would very much like a beautiful voice, if you please, sir," said the Nightingale, and the Magician waved his wand and the Nightingale found she could sing more sweetly than any other bird she had heard in the whole wide world.

"And what wish would you like to have?" said the Magician to the Kingfisher.

"I would like a new coat, if you please, sir," said the Kingfisher, and the Magician waved his wand a second time, and the Kingfisher found he was wearing a wonderful new coat of blue and green, all bright and shimmering in the sunlight, the most beautiful coat he had ever seen.

"As for you," said the Magician to the Magpie when the two other birds thanked him, "because you only pretended to find the ring I shall hide something else for you to find, and only when you find that can you have your wish," and he took a small bright thing from his pocket, and threw it into the air, and his friends the winds carried it away, no one knows where. And from that day to this the Nightingale has had the sweetest singing voice of any bird, and the Kingfisher has had a beautiful blue and green coat, but the Magpie is still searching for the bright, shining thing the Magician gave to the winds to hide. Indeed to this very day, if you leave any small bright things anywhere where the Magpie can find it, he will steal it from you, and carry it away to the Magician and ask him if this is what he hid.

But it never is, and the Magpie is still searching.

The Story of the Bullfrog

Long, long ago when the world was young, the Bullfrog was one of the most miserable of all the creatures on the earth, and one of the most conceited. He would jump along the path through the forest croaking, "How wonderful I am, how clever I am, how very clever!" until all the other creatures were tired of hearing him. He would stop any creature he met and talk to him for a long time about his cleverness, and would always end by saying, in his croaking voice, "Why has such a clever creature as I such a small body and an ugly voice? It is very unfair. Don't you think that, with my cleverness, I should be as big and strong as the Elephant, and have a loud, trumpeting voice like him?" And the other animals would say politely, "Yes, of course, Bullfrog," and hurry away in case he should start to tell them again how clever and wise he was.

The Rabbit lived in a burrow near the Bullfrog's pool and so was troubled more than the other creatures by the Bullfrog's boasting and complaining, and he decided that the

Bullfrog must be taught a lesson. So one day, when the Bullfrog said to him, "Why am I not as big and strong as the Elephant? And why haven't I a loud trumpeting voice like him? Isn't it all very unfair?" The Rabbit replied, "It is very unfair indeed, Bullfrog, and I will try to help you. There is a gnome living deep under the earth who is very wise indeed, and this afternoon I will go to visit him and ask him what you should do to become as big and strong as the Elephant and to have the loud trumpeting voice you so much wish for."

The Bullfrog was very excited, and became more boastful than ever, and told the Rabbit all over again how clever he was and how he deserved to be bigger and to have a louder voice, and hopped away towards his pool with his head held very high, dreaming of what he would do when his wish had been granted. "All the other creatures will have to listen to me then," he said to himself, "and they will admire me and tell me how clever and strong I am, and perhaps even ask me to be king instead of the Lion," and he hopped away down the path very pleased with himself.

The next day, soon after breakfast, the Bullfrog knocked on the door of the Rabbit's burrow and as soon as the Rabbit opened the door, he began to ask him questions one after the other without giving the Rabbit time to answer.

"Have you seen the gnome?" asked the Bullfrog. "What did he say? What must I do? When can I begin? Will I be as big as the Elephant soon? Tomorrow? The day after? Won't I look wonderful then? What did he say? Can I start now? Must I eat or drink a magical potion? Have you got it with you?"

"Stop, stop, stop!" said the Rabbit. "One question at a time please! Yes, I have seen the Gnome and he has told me what you must do, but it is all very secret, and before I say anything else you must promise me that you will tell nobody about it, or all the other creatures will want to become as big as elephants as well, and that would be dreadful."

"I won't tell a soul," said the Bullfrog.

"Well then," said the Rabbit, "come into my burrow and shut the door behind you, for it is a cold morning, and I will tell you what you are to do."

So the Bullfrog hopped inside the Rabbit's burrow, and sat in the Rabbit's most comfortable armchair, and listened eagerly to his instructions.

"First of all," said the Rabbit, "you must find a lonely pond, and then you must make a raft of the biggest water-lily leaf you can find, and in the middle of the night you must climb on the leaf and paddle yourself out to the middle of the pond. When you get there you must say to yourself three times, 'I am growing as big as the Elephant, and I am growing a trumpeting voice.' Then you must take the deepest breath you possibly can, and swell and swell, until you feel that you are very big indeed, and then open your mouth and imitate the Elephant's trumpeting. If you do this properly, and really feel that you are as big as an Elephant and can trumpet like him, the spell will work, and you will become very big and have a wonderful voice just as you wish. But you must not be disappointed if the spell does not work the first time, for it is a difficult spell, and may take a long time to work properly unless you are very clever indeed."

"I am sure it will work the first time," said the Bullfrog, "for I am very clever, and know just the right pond. It is not far from here. You must come and watch the spell work. We will go there together as soon as it is dark." He said goodbye to the Rabbit and hopped away from the path croaking, "How clever I am. How wonderful I am. How clever. How wonderful," until the Rabbit could hardly stop himself laughing.

That evening the Bullfrog and the Rabbit set off together for the lonely pool, dragging a huge water-lily leaf behind them, and carrying a picnic basket. "For," said the Bullfrog, "I shall be hungry when I have finished my magic and will

want something to eat." He did not offer to share his food with the Rabbit. The Rabbit said nothing, but chuckled to himself. As soon as they reached the pool, the Bullfrog helped the Rabbit push the water-lily into the water, and jumped aboard, and began to paddle towards the middle of the pond.

"Don't be frightened, Rabbit," he said. "I know that I will look very frightening when I am as big as an Elephant, and my voice will perhaps scare you, but don't run away. I shall want you to tell the other animals all about it, and tell them how brave I was, and how I looked, and what happened," and he paddled steadily out into the middle of the moonlit pond.

When he got to the middle, he sat on the leaf, and looked up at the moon and croaked, "I am growing as big as an Elephant and I am growing a loud trumpeting voice" three times, each time looking and sounding more foolish than before. Then he drew a deep breath, and swelled and swelled until the Rabbit thought he was going to burst! Just as the Rabbit thought that the Bullfrog was going to float up into the sky because he had so much air inside him, the Bullfrog opened his mouth, but the only noise that came was "Honk! Honk!" very different from the magnificent trumpeting of the Elephant, and the Bullfrog nearly fell off the water-lily with surprise and annoyance, and the Rabbit nearly suffocated through trying not to laugh.

"Try again," shouted the Rabbit, "I am sure you nearly managed it that time. After all it is a very difficult spell and you must not expect to succeed the first time."

"I was only practising that time," said the Bullfrog rather crossly, "I will do it properly now."

And he said three times, "I am growing as big as an Elephant, and growing a loud trumpeting voice," and breathed in very deeply, and swelled and swelled and swelled until his eyes nearly popped out of his head and he looked so ridiculous that the Rabbit had to put both paws over his mouth to stop himself from laughing. Then just as the Rabbit felt sure that he could not swell anymore without bursting, the Bullfrog opened his mouth very wide indeed, and thought very hard indeed of himself as being as big as an Elephant, and tried to trumpet, but the only sound he made was

"Honk! Honk!" just as before, and he nearly fell off the water-lily leaf with annoyance and surprise.

"Third time lucky," called the Rabbit who was nearly helpless with laughter, for the Bullfrog looked very funny, and the Bullfrog repeated the words again, drew an even deeper breath, and swelled and swelled like a balloon, and opened his mouth as wide as he could, but again all that he said was "Honk! Honk!"

And so it went on through the whole night, and it was a very tired and crestfallen Bullfrog that hopped back towards his home in the morning, though he said that he would try again the following night.

"It is a very difficult spell, Rabbit," he said, "and only a very clever and brave creature like myself would dare to try it. I am sure that after a little while I shall make it work. No one else could, but I am cleverer than other creatures." He hopped away to his home saying to himself, "How wonderful I am. How clever I am," until all the other creatures (whom the Rabbit had told about his joke) could hardly stop laughing.

But the Bullfrog did not notice that people were laughing at him, and went to the pond again the very next night and tried all over again, but whenever he opened his mouth, however much he swelled, all that came out was "Honk! Honk! Honk!"

He tried again the night after that, and the one after that, and every night afterwards except when it was winter and the pond was covered with ice, but he never became as big as an Elephant, and the only sound he ever made was "Honk! Honk! Honk!" and he is still trying, to this very day. Indeed if, on a warm summer night, you happen to go near the pond where the Bullfrog tries his spell, you will hear him going "Honk! Honk! Honk! Honk!" all the night long, and you may even, if you look very carefully, see him swelling himself up until it looks as if he is going to burst. And I would not be surprised if you heard the Rabbit still laughing.

The Story of
the Cat

Once upon a time, when the world was young, the Cat decided that she would like to learn to sing, for she was very envious of all the birds who had such sweet voices, and very cross because all the creatures laughed at her when she tried to imitate them. The Cat was a very proud animal and hated to think that anybody could do anything that she could not. In fact she would never admit that any other creature was prettier or wiser or more clever than she, which annoyed all the birds and animals very much.

One day she met the Rabbit, who was busy planting some lettuce in the garden in front of his burrow, and said to him, "Hello, Rabbit, have you seen the Nightingale anywhere?"

"I haven't seen her in a long time," said the Rabbit. "She is so very shy that she only leaves her nest to sing in the middle of the night when I am fast asleep. Why do you want to see her?"

"Although I have, as you know, a very beautiful voice," said the Cat, "I thought that I might ask the Nightingale how

I could make it even more beautiful than it is at present, for she sings so sweetly that she must be able to tell me what I must do."

"There is no need to look for the Nightingale," said the Rabbit. "My friend the Gnome who lives deep under the surface of the earth has told me of a way to give any creature, even one who cannot sing at all, a most beautiful voice. That is why I myself am able to sing so well," (for the Rabbit, at this time, had a beautiful singing voice himself).

"Do tell me about it, please, Rabbit," said the Cat.

So the Rabbit stopped planting lettuce and invited the Cat into his burrow, and when they were both comfortable, said,

"Not far from here is a magic well. If you were to swim in this well at midnight you would find that you would get a most beautiful singing voice. You can swim, can't you?" he added.

"I have never tried to swim before," said the Cat, "but I am so clever that I am sure I could if I tried."

"Then we will go to the well together this very night," said the Rabbit. "And then tomorrow you will sing even more sweetly than the Nightingale."

And so they agreed to meet at the hollow oak just as the sun was setting, and the Rabbit promised the Cat that he would take her to the magic well.

That evening, just as the sun was setting, the Rabbit and the Cat set out together. They walked through the forest until they came to an old well hidden in the middle of a thicket of briars.

"Here we are," said the Rabbit. "Now all you have to do is jump into the well, and swim about for a little time, and then you will be able to sing more beautifully than any other creature in the whole wide world."

"The well is very deep," said the Cat.

"You are so very brave and clever that you need not worry about that," said the Rabbit. "A cowardly animal might be afraid, but I know that you are not."

"Yes, of course," said the Cat. "The water looks very cold," she added.

"You are too brave and strong to bother about that," said the Rabbit. "An animal less brave and clever might be afraid, but I know that you are not."

"Of course not," said the Cat, and she climbed nervously onto the wall of the well. "Is it midnight yet?" asked the Cat.

"It is exactly midnight," said the Rabbit.

"Then I'd better jump in," said the Cat.

"Yes," said the Rabbit, and gave the poor Cat a push!

Down she fell, down, down, down, down, and hit the water with a tremendous splash. The water was very cold and dark and deep, and the Cat sank straight to the bottom, for she did not know how to swim. She swallowed a great deal of water, and was very frightened indeed, but just as she thought she was going to drown, she heard the Rabbit calling, "Catch hold of this," and a rope came falling down into the water. So she held on to the rope, and the Rabbit pulled her out, more dead than alive.

"Now," said the Rabbit, "you must try to sing," and the Cat opened her mouth but there came out only the most dreadful yowl. It was so dreadful that the Rabbit put both his paws over his ears as he ran away home before the Cat found out that she had been tricked.

The Cat never quite forgave the Rabbit for this trick, though she was still determined to sing, and asked every bird she met where the Nightingale was to be found, and if someone would introduce her to her. But all the birds laughed and flew away. So the Cat tried to learn to sing all by herself, for she was far too proud to admit that she couldn't ever hope to sing as sweetly as a bird. And from that day to this you can see the Cat in the garden trying to creep close enough to any birds that are nearby to ask them where the Nightingale lives, and you can see the birds fly away twittering with laughter. And the Cat is still trying to learn to sing, and you may hear her very often in the middle of the night making a most dreadful noise. And to this very day she is afraid of water.

The Story of
the Donkey

In the very beginning of things, when all the animals and birds were friendly with each other, the Donkey had a most beautiful voice. He was very proud of his voice, and used to sing to himself and to all the other animals from morning till night. His greatest friend was the Rabbit who also was a very fine singer, and whenever the animals had a concert the Donkey and the Rabbit would sing duets, one after another until the paws and hooves of all the other animals were quite sore from clapping them.

One day, however, the Rabbit and the Donkey were asked to give a very special concert at the Lion's den, because it was the Lion's birthday. They were very pleased about this, and practised very hard for the great occasion. They would meet every morning and sing together in the forest far away from all the other animals, so that no one should know what songs they were going to sing at the concert. They wanted to give the Lion and his guests a big surprise.

It was just seven days before the day of the concert that the awful thing happened. The Donkey and the Rabbit had been practising all day, and had not noticed the thunder-clouds rolling up, and had been singing so loudly that they had not heard the thunder grumbling, "I'm coming, I'm coming, it's going, it's going, it's going to rain." So that when the rain came they were taken by surprise, and got soaking wet, for they had been very silly animals and had not taken their mackintoshes and umbrellas with them. They both arrived at the Donkey's home in a very bedraggled condition, and were so tired that they went to bed immediately, without even stopping to fill hot water bottles, or dry themselves properly.

The next morning when they woke up the Rabbit turned to the Donkey and was just going to cry, "Wake up. It's time we had our breakfast," when he found that he could not speak. He had lost his voice. He was very frightened. He pulled the Donkey's ears to make him wake up too. At last the Donkey opened his eyes and was just going to say, "Leave me alone. It isn't time to get up yet," when he found that he had lost his voice as well. The two animals looked at one another in horror. Where had their voices gone? They looked high and low, all over their little home, but could not find them anywhere. At last the Donkey scraped up a patch of dust and wrote in it with his hoof:

WE MUST ASK OWL HE WIL NO

(The Donkey was not very good at spelling.) So both the animals set off to look for the Owl.

They found him at last sitting outside his home in the Old Hollow Oak, half asleep in the bright morning sun. The Rabbit tried to say, "Good morning, Owl," but of course he had lost his voice and could not say anything at all. The Donkey tried to say, "We have lost our voices, Owl," but he could not make a sound. So both the animals jumped up and down, and the Rabbit waved his paws, and the Donkey clapped his hooves together, to draw the Owl's attention. After a while the Owl woke up and said rather crossly, "Wo-o-o-oo-o" and then "What a too-doo," and promptly fell asleep again. The two animals did not know what to do. Then the Donkey remembered how he had written in the dust earlier that day, and so started to collect grasses and twigs, making faces at the Rabbit to try and tell him what he was doing. The Rabbit soon understood, and very carefully the two animals laid twigs and bits of grass on the ground to make up letters, and when they had done, it spelt out (rather crookedly):

WE HAVE LOZT OWR VOICES
WERE CAN WE FIND THEM

and then the Donkey, as an afterthought for he was a very polite animal, added:

PLEEZE OWL

Then they both jumped about and clapped their paws and hooves together again until the Owl woke up and saw what they had done. When the Owl had read the words on the ground he looked even more solemn than usual, and sat and thought for a long time. Indeed he sat and thought for such a long time that both the Donkey and the Rabbit thought he had fallen asleep again, and were just beginning to jump about and wave their legs again, when the Owl opened one yellow eye and said, "I will tell you what to do-o-o. Yo-o-ou must go across the Co-o-o-ld Mountains, to the Land of the Shadows, and when you get there you must follow the path across the m-o-o-o-r until you come to a h-u-u-u-ge cave. That is the h-o-o-o-o-me of the King of all the Spiders, and if you go into the cave very quietly, taking great care not to touch any of the spiders' webs, or twitch your long ears against them you will find in another cave inside the bigger one, a cupboard labelled 'Voices.' You must open the cupboard, and there you will find your voices for that is where all the lost voices are taken by the Spiders. Pick up your two-o-o voices—and take care that they are your own voices and not some other animals'—and come out again as quietly as before. If you make a sound, and wake up the Spiders, they will take your voices from you-o-o and you-o-o will never se-eee them again."

So the Rabbit and the Donkey set out on their journey. The path to the Cold Mountains was very long and very tiring. The Rabbit's little paws soon got tired, and he had to stop the Donkey by pulling at his tail, and then climb on his back. After a very, very long time they came to the Cold Mountains and climbed and climbed and climbed until they thought they could climb no farther. Just as they were giving up all hope of ever seeing the Land of the Shadows and getting their voices back again, they found that they had reached a big cave in the mountain side. They went into the cave, and found that it was not really a cave at all, but a long tunnel, and after they had walked along the tunnel for a little time they found themselves at the other side of the mountain, and looking down into a valley that was very grey and covered in mist.

They climbed down into the valley, and after a while, found the crooked path that led across the moors. It was now nearly night-time so they both lay down in the heather, the Rabbit curled up between the Donkey's four feet, and fell fast asleep, for they were very tired.

When they woke up the next day they lost no time in starting their journey across the moor, and very soon they came to a huge cave in the side of a tall mountain, and on the outside of the cave there was a notice which they could only just read because of the swirling mist. It said:

```
THE KING OF THE SPIDERS
       LIVES HERE

       KEEP OUT

   NO VOICES RETURNED
   WITHOUT AUTHORITY

       TRESPASSERS
   WILL BE PROSECUTED
```

They crept into the cave very, very quietly. There were spiders' webs everywhere—on the walls, on the roof, and most of all, on the big wooden throne where the biggest of all Spiders, with a gold crown on his head and bright red shoes on all of his eight feet, sat fast asleep. Hardly daring to breathe, they tiptoed past the throne into the second cave, the Donkey taking care not to twitch his ears, and the Rabbit walking on the very tips of his four tired little paws. In the second cave, just as the Owl had said, there was a cupboard.

Now the Rabbit became so excited he could hardly stand still. The Donkey opened the cupboard door, and there on a shelf were lots and lots of voices, big ones, small ones, thin ones, round ones, rough ones, smooth ones, and even baby ones. The Donkey picked up the voice labelled "DONKEY: RECENT ADDITION" in his mouth. The Rabbit could not reach the high shelf, and jumped about excitedly, forgetting all about keeping quiet, trying to make the Donkey hand him his own voice as well. The Donkey was so excited that he paid no attention to the Rabbit at all but turned round and ran towards the mouth of the cave. He made such a noise, however, that the Spiders all woke up, and very quickly spread their webs across his way, so that the Donkey, running very fast, fell and dropped his voice, and it rolled out in front of him out of the cave and hit a rock and broke. The Donkey was very strong and escaped from the Spiders (who were only trying to get the voice back, really, and did not want to hurt him) and picked up his broken voice and ran all the way through the mists across the Land of the Shadows and through the tunnel, and did not stop until he reached home. The Rabbit, who had crawled under the webs and escaped in the scuffle, ran after him. But ever since that day the Donkey's voice has been broken, for no one could mend it, and the poor little Rabbit has no voice at all.

ABOUT THE AUTHOR AND ILLUSTRATOR

Robin Skelton, former Chairman of the Creative Writing Department at the University of Victoria, is renowned for his writing in many different styles. His previous book for children is I am Me.

Pamela Breeze Currie worked as an artist and designer in Manchester for many years. She now continues her career as a freelance children's book illustrator in Edinburgh.